U0130162

红 妆 绿 抹

刘 乐 君 的 五 彩 世 界

Dressing In Red and Green
—— Liu Lejun’s Antique Colorful World

从传统到个性

——陶瓷是人们之间交流和联系的纽带

——从传统到现代陶瓷精神价值的变化

——关于延续、尊重和景仰传统

在乐君的艺术世界中，我能看到作品的形式主要是为装饰服务的，装饰是作者的艺术动机，其主要体现在少量的图案部分上。作品的灵感来源于自然和色彩，而作品的重点却是在诠释创造一个更加丰富的“自然”。乐君在传统釉上绘画色彩上注入了当代语言表现形式，这给予了其陶瓷作品的时代价值，她模仿自然，却不是简单地再现自然，作品中色彩的运用显示了乐君作品的想法和理念，它是一种对自然的诠释，但却以景仰和尊重传统为前提。

白雪和寒冷是我对冬季的感受和经历，植物不再生长，树上没有树叶。而在景德镇我却没有遇过这样的冬天，树上总挂满树叶和绿色。在乐君的作品中有许多关于季节的暗示，我能看到这里有她熟悉的春天、夏天和秋季。在这些自然风景中，作品还增添了她的内心风景，这些被认为代表过去，而真实的自我感受被呈现在陶瓷这个媒介中。

我可以看到作品在物象和形式间存在的一种强有力联系，我看到用内心描绘的花、枝叶和鸟儿们，这更贴近自然，这就是我的体会。

我们从来没有放弃。当乐君将自然转换为陶瓷，她也给了我一种对生活状况的解释。一位中国艺术历史学教授曾经对我说过：如果自然是干净和清心的，我们的生活也是美好的。对于乐君的陶瓷作品这应是客观的评价。相信陶瓷是你我间超越时间和空间的、自由和敞开心扉的对话，是人们间情感交流和连接的纽带。

查尔斯·米歇尔森

挪威卑尔根国立艺术学院设计系教授

From traditional to personal

—Porcelain as communication and connection between people.
—From traditional porcelain, to change of values.
—About continuity; respect and admiration for tradition.

In Lejun' s artwork, I can see forms whose function and main purpose are for decoration. The physical object has the motive area and the smaller pattern area.

There are motives from the nature, with colours that emphasis her interpretation to create a richness of the nature. The colour chart Lejun has created for the over glaze painting add a more contemporary expression, which give her porcelain work values of our time.

She imitates the nature, more than she tries to copy the nature. The colour chart carries Lejun' s concept and interpretation. It' s an interpretation of Lejun view to the nature but still it' s also an admiration to the tradition.

My winter experience is snow, cold, no plants growing and no leaves on the trees. In Jingdezhen I have never recognized winter as I know it. I can always see some leaves on the trees. In Lejun' s porcelain object I recognize in the motive—the season, there are many sign in her object of time and site. I can see she is most familiar with spring, summer and fall. She adds her inner landscape to the painting of the nature. It' s recognized and represented as past and true personal interpretation presented in the porcelain medium.

By this work, she has a very strong conceptual connection between physical and surface form. We can see branches with flowers and birds and by let the branch is described on the inside too; the branch is stretched out in the air. That' s closer to the nature, and how I have experienced the theme.

We never give up and when Lejun transform the nature to the porcelain she also give me statement about living condition. A Chinese art historian professor said to me : If the nature is clean and fresh , our life condition is good.

I think this is valid for Lejun porcelain. To believe on porcelain as a time capsule with space for a free and open dialog. To use porcelain as object for communication and connection between people.

Charles Mikhalsen
Professor of Bergen Academy of the Fine Arts (Norway)

刘乐君 女，生于景德镇，美术学硕士，景德镇陶瓷学院科技艺术学院副教授，景德镇陶瓷学院科技艺术学院陶瓷设计教研室主任，江西省美术家协会会员，景德镇女陶艺家协会理事。

近年参展及学术交流：

2001年 9月　第一届全国陶瓷艺术与设计展览和评比《叶》　入选奖

2003年 9月　第二届全国陶瓷艺术展览《合声》　铜奖　北京

2006年 4月　江西省第四届青年美术作品展《天圆地方》　一等奖　南昌

2006年10月　第八届全国陶瓷艺术创新评比《一泓清碧映荷花》铜奖

2007年 6月　景德镇陶瓷学院中国美术馆陶艺作品展　北京中国美术馆

2008年 1月　第三届现代手工艺提名展　上海双城画廊

2008年 1月-3月　挪威卑尔根国立艺术学院（Bergen National Academy of the Arts，Norway）访问学者

2008年 6月　德化中韩陶艺邀请展　福建德化

2008年 8月　三国演义·2008年中日韩现代陶艺新世代交流展　佛山石湾

2008年10月　第五届景德镇陶瓷评比百花奖《一泓清碧映荷花之三》　铜奖

2008年10月　第五届景德镇陶瓷评比百花奖《十二花卉之古彩大盘》　铜奖

2008年12月　江西省青年艺术设计双年展　二等奖　南昌

2009年 5月　中国景德镇陶瓷艺术作品展　联合国教科文组织总部　法国巴黎（Paris）

2009年 9月　第13届上海艺术博览会

2009年10月　江西省第十二届青年美术作品展　优秀奖　南昌

2010年 6月　江西省第六届青年美术作品展　二等奖　南昌

论著：

2005年10月《传统陶瓷古彩装饰》　武汉理工大学出版社

2009年 1月　《综合材料艺术实验》　武汉理工大学出版社

2009年 6月　《AutoCAD基础教程》　北京工艺美术出版社

Liu Lejun

Born in Jingdezhen in 1978, gained MFA degree of Fine arts in JDZ Ceramic Institute in 2003. Associate Professor and director of section of ceramic art design in fine art department in Jingdezhen science and technology art Institute, a member of Jiangxi Artists Association and a member of Jingdezhen Female Ceramic Artists Association.

Exhibition and awards in recent years:

2001, The 1st National Ceramic Art and Design Exhibition in Beijing, 《leaf》, Selected work

2003, The 2nd National Ceramic Art and Design Exhibition in Beijing, 《Singing in harmony》, Bronze Award

2006, The 4th Youth Fine Art Exhibition of Jiangxi Province, 《Round sky and Quare earth》,Gold Award, Nanchang

2006, The 8th National Ceramic Art Creativity Competition, 《Lotus flower standing in the blue river》, Bronze Award

2007, Teacher' s Ceramic Works Exhibition of Jingdezhen Ceramic Institute in National Art Museum Of China, Beijing

2008, The 3rd Modern Nomination Handicrafts Exhibition in Shanghai, Shuangcheng

2008, Jan 18–Feb 10, as the artist and teacher take part in the course of "Image and Message" in Bergen National Academy of Arts in Norway.

2008, China and South Korea Ceramic Artist Invitation Exhibition in Fujian, Dehua

2008, The Performance of Three Kingdoms. 2008 China, Japan and South Korea New Century Contemporary Pottery Art Exhibition in Foshan

2008, The 5th Jingdezhen "Baihua" Ceramics Exhibition 《the lotus flower standing in the green pond No.3》,Bronze Award

2008, The 5th Jingdezhen "Baihua" Ceramics Exhibition 《12 flower of Antique–color plate》, Bronze Award

2008, Dec, Jiangxi Province Youth Art Design Biennial Exhibition in Nanchang, Second Prize

2009, "Jingdezhen Ceramics Works Exhibition", in UNESC, Paris, France

2009, The 12th Jiangxi Fine Art Exhihition in Nanchang for young artist

2010, The 6th Jiangxi Fine Art Exhihition in Nanchang for young artist, Sliver Prize

Books Published:

2005, 《Traditional Ancient Color Ceramic Ornament》 Wuhan University of Technology Press Awarded the first prize of the 2nd Jiangxi province teaching book

2009, 《Composite Materials Art Experiment》 Wuhan University of Technology Press

清荷一
Fragrance of Lotus Flower NO.1
瓷、木板
1330℃还原，760℃粉彩
105cm×45cm×3cm
2007年

清荷二
Fragrance of Lotus Flower NO.2
瓷、木板
1330℃还原，760℃粉彩
105cm×45cm×3cm
2007年

清荷三
Fra grance of Lotus Flower NO.3
瓷、木板
1330℃还原，760℃粉彩
105cm×45cm×3cm
2007年

清荷四
Fragrance of Lotus Flower NO.4
瓷、木板
1330℃还原，760℃粉彩
105cm×45cm×3cm
2007年

红梅鹦哥图（局部）
Plum and Parakeets Porcelain（Partial）

红梅鹦哥图
Plum and Parakeets
瓷
1330℃还原，790℃低温古彩
53cm×36cm×36cm
2009年

茶花蛱蝶（局部）
Camellia and Butterfly（Partial）

茶花蛱蝶
Camellia and Butterfly
瓷
1330℃还原，790℃古彩
8cm×45cm×45cm
2006年

碧桃蛱蝶
Flowering Peach and Butterfly
瓷
1330℃还原，790℃古彩
9cm×48cm×48cm
2007年

碧桃蛱蝶（局部）
Flowering Peach and Butterfly（Partial）

大丽花开一
Dahlia Blooming NO.1
1330℃还原，790℃古彩
33cm×33cm×50cm
2007年

大丽花开二
Dahlia Blooming NO.2
瓷
1330℃还原，790℃古彩
31cm×31cm×52cm
2008年

大丽花开二（局部）
Dahlia Blooming NO.2（Partial）

富贵大丽一
Poised Dahlia NO.1
瓷
1330℃还原，790℃古彩
59cm×45cm×45cm
2009年

富贵大丽二
Poised Dahlia NO.2
瓷
1330℃还原，790℃古彩
59cm×45cm×45cm
2009年

富贵大丽三
Poised Dahlia NO.3
瓷
1330℃还原，790℃古彩
59cm×45cm×45cm
2009年

荷花蜻蜓（局部）
Lotus Flower and Dragonfly（Partial）

荷花蜻蜓
Lotus Flower and Dragonfly
瓷
1330℃还原，770℃粉彩
28cm×28cm×4cm
2005年

梅花鹦鹉图
Plum and Parrot
瓷
1330℃还原，790℃古彩
31cm×31cm×28cm
2009年

木芙蓉
Hibiscus
瓷
1330℃还原，790℃古彩
45cm×45cm×6cm
2006年

夏月荷塘
Moon Hanging Over the Lotus Pond in Summer
瓷、本金
1330℃还原，790℃古彩
48cm×48cm×8cm
2009年

喜上眉梢
Eyes Twinkle with Pleasure
瓷
1330℃还原，790℃古彩
34cm×31cm×31cm
2008年

木槿蛱蝶
Hibiscus and butterfly
瓷、木板
1330℃还原，790℃古彩
55cm×28cm×28cm
2007年

石竹花
Pink Flowers
瓷
1330℃还原，790℃古彩
19cm×22cm×19cm
2004年

秋蜓野草图
Dragonfly and Wild Grass
瓷
1330℃还原，790℃低温古彩
56cm×41cm×41cm
2006年

细草蛱蝶图
Wild Grass and Butterfly
瓷
1330℃还原，790℃古彩
49cm×32cm
2009年

木芙蓉花一
Hibiscus NO.1
瓷、本金
1330℃还原，760℃粉彩
24cm×24cm
2008年

木芙蓉花二
Hibiscus NO.2
瓷、本金
1330℃还原，760℃粉彩
24cm×24cm
2008年

碧桃花
Peach Blossom
瓷
1320℃还原，780℃古彩
46cm×36cm
2009年

初冬畫

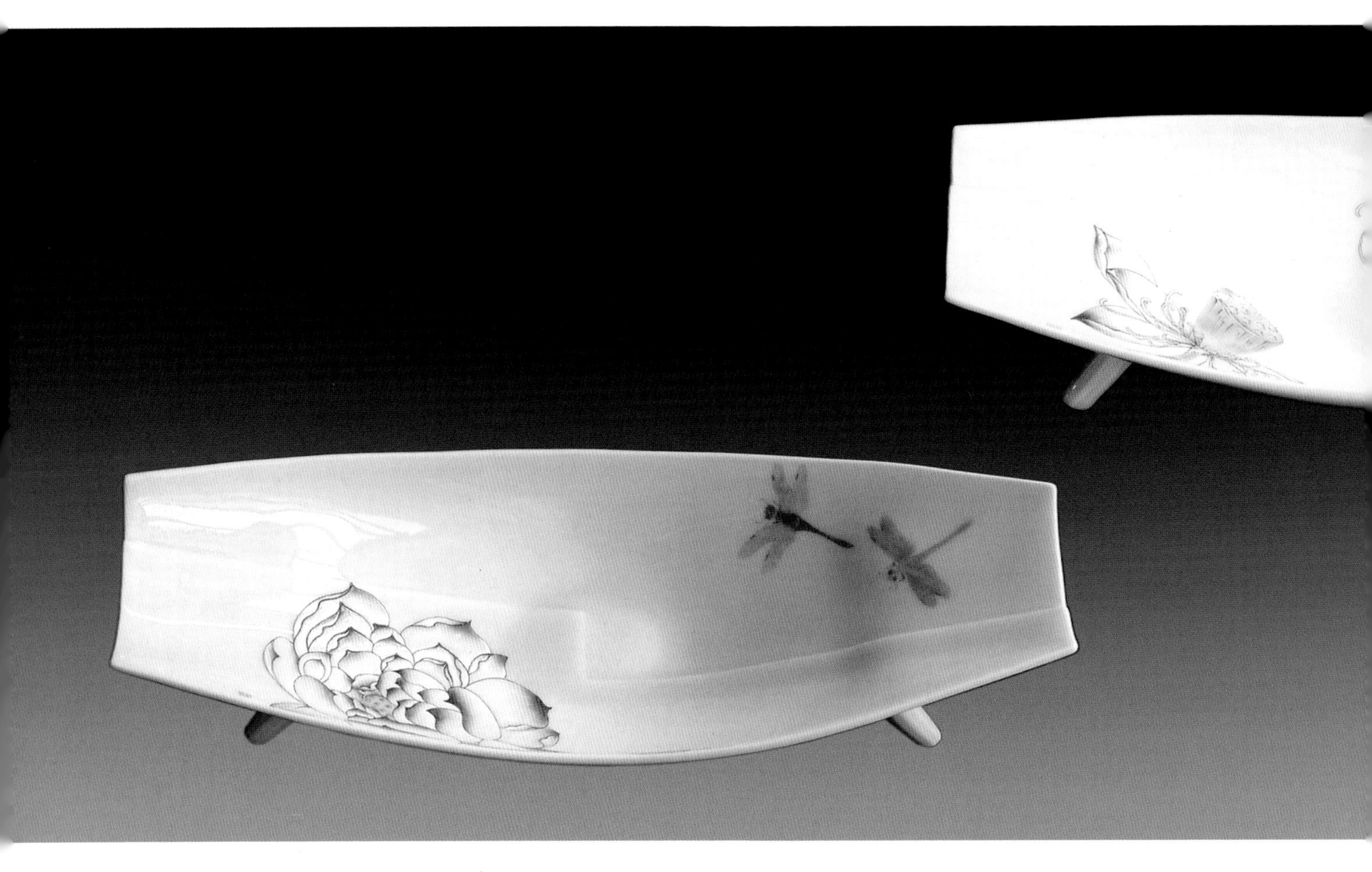

一泓青碧映荷花
Lotus Flower Standing in Green Water
瓷
1330℃还原，770℃粉彩
132cm×45cm×15cm
2008年

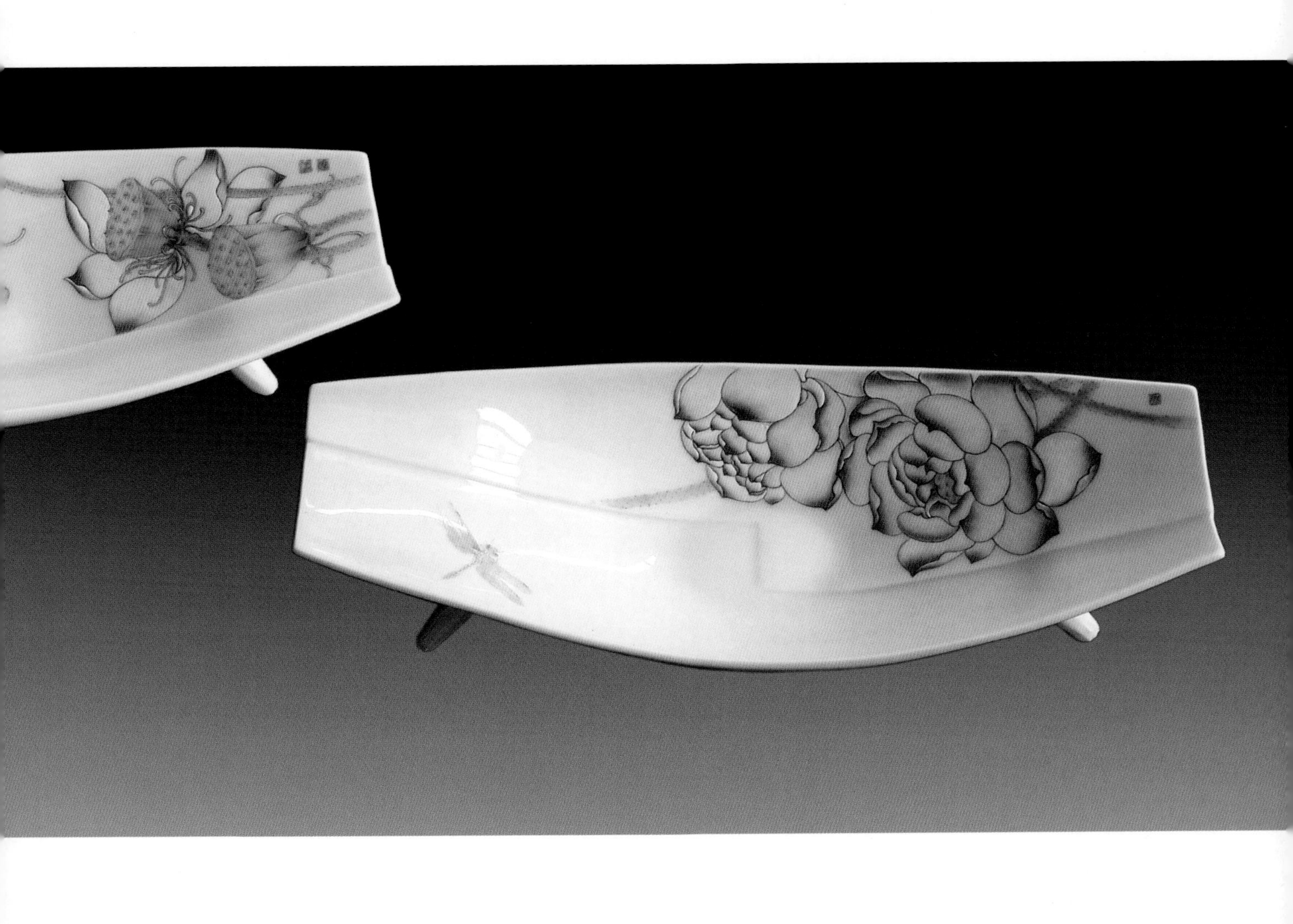

茶蘼花馥一
Fragrance of Rosa Rubus Flower NO.1
瓷
1330℃还原，790℃古彩
8cm×48cm×48cm
2008年

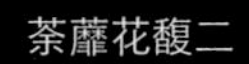
荼蘼花馥二

Fragrance of Rosa Rubus Flower NO.2

瓷

1330℃还原，790℃古彩

8cm×48cm×48cm

2008年

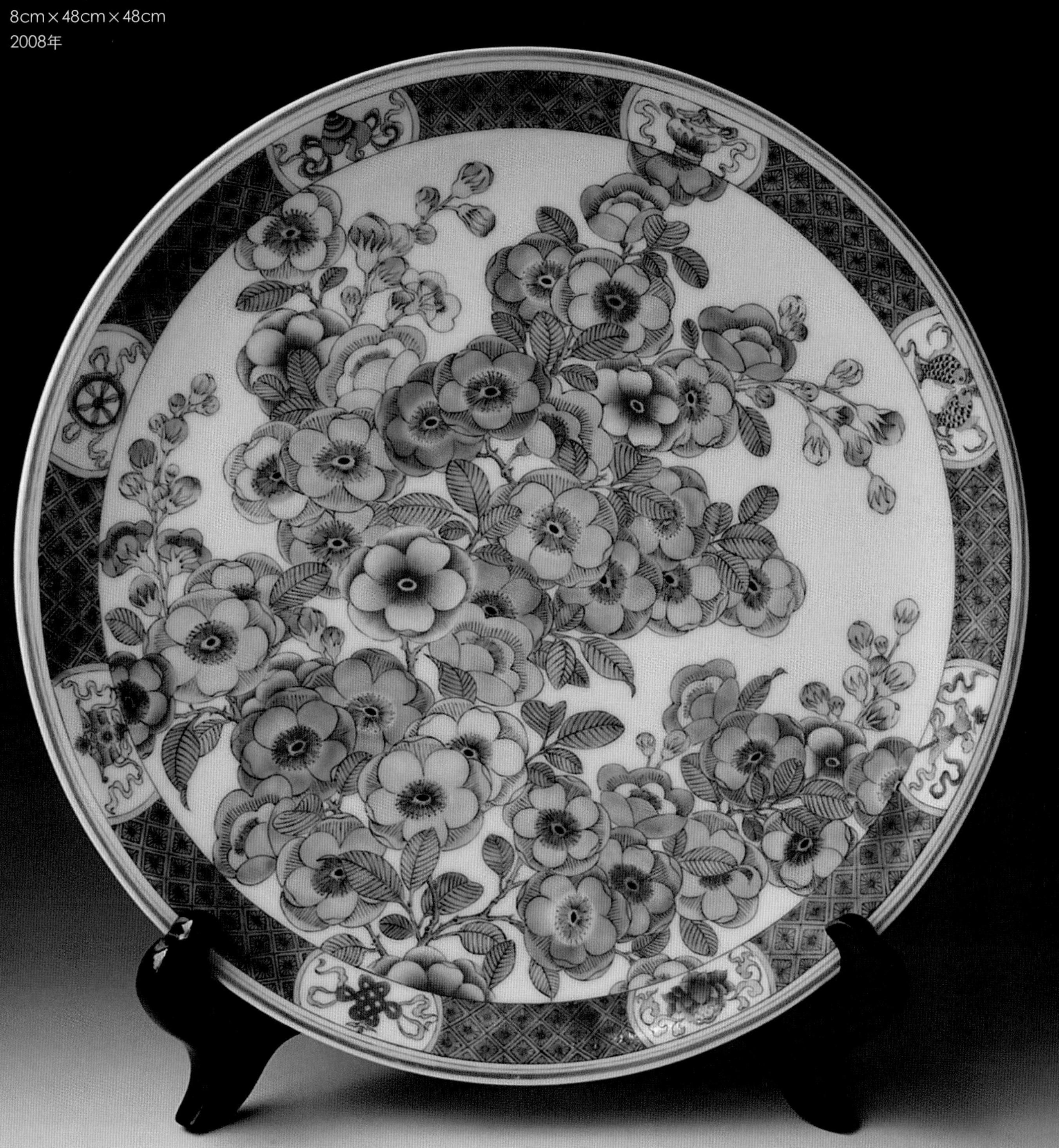

石竹花开
Pink Flowers Blooming
瓷
1330℃还原，790℃古彩
42cm×29cm×29cm
2006年

2006年

秋葵一
Okra NO.1
瓷
1330℃还原，790℃古彩
27cm×27cm×58cm
2005年

秋葵二（局部）
Okra NO.2（Partial）

秋葵蛱蝶图
Okra and Butterfly
瓷
1330℃还原，790℃古彩
7cm×45cm×45cm
2005年

荷塘清音
Birds Whisper Over the Lotus Pond
瓷
1330℃还原，780℃古彩
32cm×32cm×51cm
2010年

凭窗　Leaning on the Window　瓷
1330℃还原，790℃古彩
9cm×8cm×14cm　2009年

憩瓷　Having a Rest　瓷
1330℃还原，790℃古彩
8cm×12cm×7cm　2009年

绿梅　Green Plum　瓷
1330℃还原，790℃古彩
12cm×15cm×8cm　2009年

山菊花　Wild Chrysanthemum　瓷
1330℃还原，790℃古彩
9cm×12cm×9cm　2009年

赏　Appreciating　瓷
1330℃还原，790℃古彩
9cm×12cm×8cm　2009年

静待君来　Waiting for Back　瓷
1330℃还原，790℃古彩
10cm×2cm×8cm　2009年

牡丹蛱蝶　Chinese Peony and Butterfly　瓷
1330℃还原，790℃古彩
10cm×15cm×8cm　2009年

秋草图　Grass in the Autumn　瓷
1330℃还原，790℃古彩
9cm×2cm×8cm　2009年

芙蓉　Hibiscus　瓷
1330℃还原，790℃古彩
7cm×13cm×9cm　2009年

野趣　The Landscape of Outside　瓷
1330℃还原，790℃古彩
10cm×12cm×8cm　2009年

钓　Fishing　瓷
1330℃还原，790℃古彩
10cm×15cm×8cm　2009年

春桃花　Plum Blossoming in the Spring　瓷
1330℃还原，790℃古彩
10cm×15cm×7cm　2009年

图书在版编目(CIP)数据

深度追踪中国当代实力派陶艺家／李砚祖主编.－南昌：江西美术出版社，2010.11
ISBN 978-7-5480-0447-9

Ⅰ.①深…　Ⅱ.①李…　Ⅲ.①陶瓷－工艺美术－作品集－中国－现代　Ⅳ.①J527

中国版本图书馆CIP数据核字（2010）第204401号

深度追踪中国当代实力派陶艺家
SHENDU ZHUIZONG ZHONGGUO DANGDAI SHILIPAI TAOYIJIA

出版发行：江西美术出版社
地　　址：南昌市子安路66号
网　　址：www.jxfinearts.com
E－mail：jxms@jxpp.com
经　　销：新华书店
印　　刷：深圳市森广源实业发展有限公司
开　　本：889mm×1194mm　1/16
印　　张：15
版　　次：2010年11月第1版
印　　次：2010年11月第1次印刷
印　　数：5000
书　　号：ISBN 978-7-5480-0447-9
定　　价：120.00元（全套五本）

赣版权登字—06—2010—265